Beautiful, Little Black
true beauty from the coils in your hair to
the bend of your toes.

You are my Joy

I Love You ♡

You are Amazing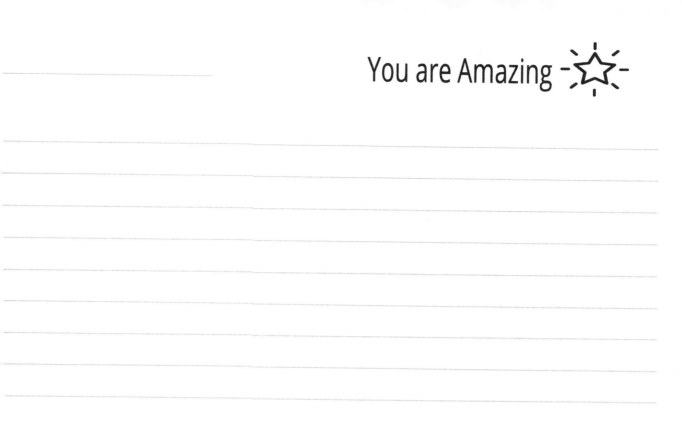

You are my Sunshine

I Am Proud of You ♡

I Am Proud of You ♡

You are my shinning star

You are the Future-☆-

You are fearfully and wonderfully made"
Psalm 139:14 (Perfectly made)

You are Enough

You are needed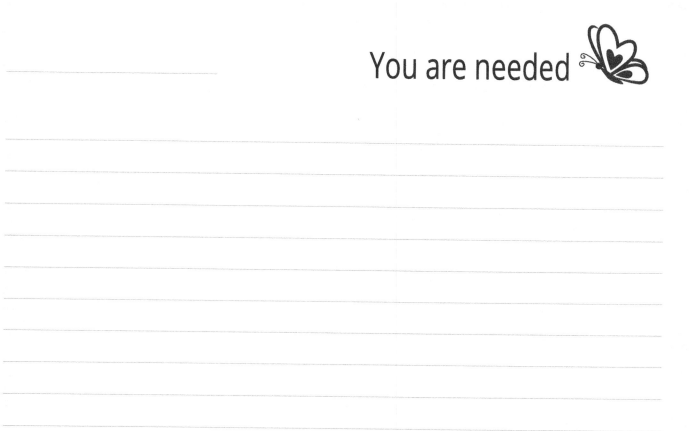

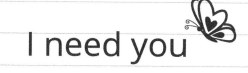
I need you

In you, I see Legacy

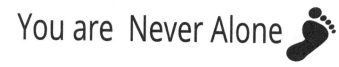

You are Never Alone

You are Capable ☆

You are unique

Love yourself ♡

You are Phenomenal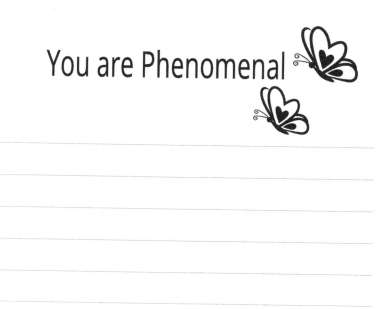

You are Resilient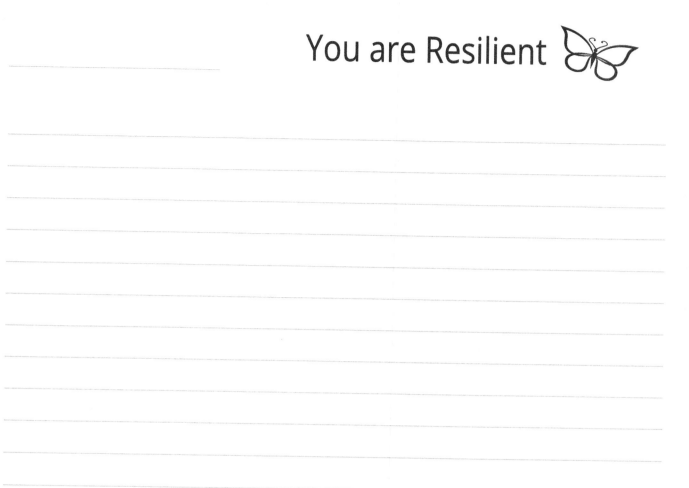

You are more precious than diamonds and rubies

Proverb 3:15

In you there is Purpose ☆

Your smile warms my heart ⭐

You are an Answered Prayer

You are Brilliant

My Sweet Princess, you are Priceless

You are Extraordinary ☆

You are Creative

I love you ♡

I love you ♡

I love you ♡

You are Important

I am Proud of you

I am Proud of you

Be Grateful ☆

You are a Blessing -☆-

You can do all things through Christ
Philippian 4:13

You are Kind
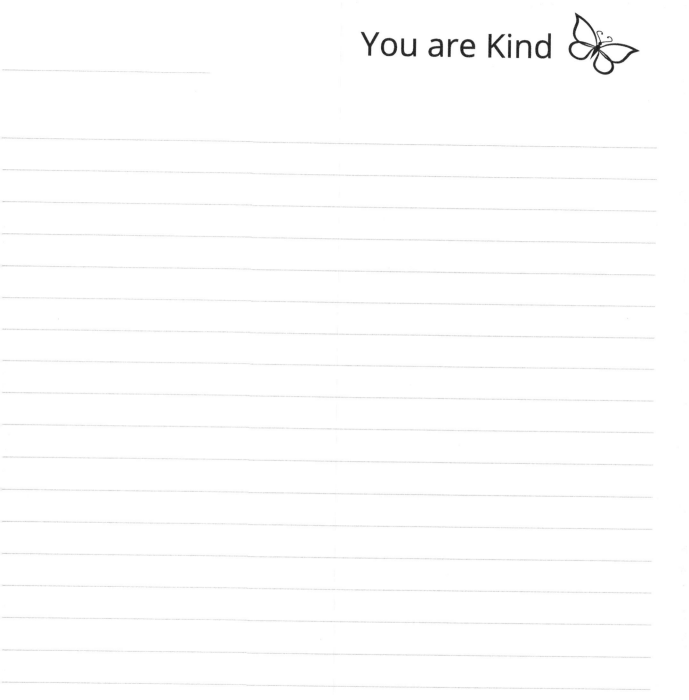

You are Smart -☆-

You are a Genius

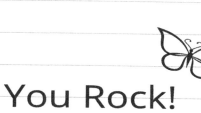
You Rock!

You will Succeed ☆

I Believe in you

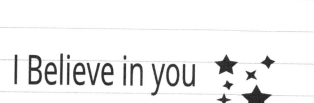

I Believe in you

You Matter

You are Necessary

You are my Joy

You are my Joy

You are Courageous -☆-

You are Powerful

Hello Princess

You are Chosen

You are Precious

You are Victorious

You are Gifted

You are Radiant

I love you ♡

I am Proud of you

Made in the USA
Middletown, DE
14 July 2024

57285834R00057